Bunnies and Their Hobbies

Bunnies and Their Hobbies

After a long day at work,

by *Nancy Carlson*

PUFFIN BOOKS

bunnies come home,

PUFFIN BOOKS

Viking Penguin Inc., 40 West 23rd Street, New York, New York 10010, U.S.A.
Penguin Books Ltd, Harmondsworth, Middlesex, England
Penguin Books Australia Ltd, Ringwood, Victoria, Australia
Penguin Books Canada Limited, 2801 John Street, Markham, Ontario, Canada L3R 1B4
Penguin Books (N.Z.) Ltd, 182–190 Wairau Road, Auckland 10, New Zealand

First published by Carolrhoda Books Inc. 1984
Published in Picture Puffins 1985

Printed in the United States of America by
General Offset Co., Inc., Jersey City, New Jersey
Set in Goudy Old Style

Library of Congress Cataloging in Publication Data
Carlson, Nancy L.   Bunnies and their hobbies.
"Puffin books."
Summary: Describes the many activities bunnies like to
spend their time on after "a long day at work."
1. Children's stories, American.   [1. Rabbits—Fiction.
2. Hobbies—Fiction]   I. Title.
PZ7.C21665Bu   1985   [E]   84-26458   ISBN 0 14 050.538 5

change their clothes,

To Uncle Bill and his hobbies, Aunt Char, and
all our great times at the lake

eat dinner,

and do the dishes.
Then it's time for
bunnies and their hobbies.

Some bunnies like to do a little yardwork
in the evenings.

Others would rather sunbathe.

Bunnies who appreciate dance
may go to an aerobic dance class
or learn the latest steps
at Arthur Murray.

Bowling is a favorite hobby of many bunnies.
So is playing cards.

Artistic bunnies paint pictures
or go to museums.
Musical bunnies play instruments.

Concerned bunnies often volunteer
to help others.

Many bunnies are collectors.
Some collect stamps.
Others collect aluminum cans.

Handy bunnies build things,
like birdhouses.

Romantic bunnies like to fall in love.

It's not uncommon to find outdoor bunnies
fishing or playing soccer.

Quiet bunnies prefer to read a book
or doze in a favorite chair.

Different bunnies enjoy different hobbies,
but when bedtime comes,
all bunnies like to go to sleep.

Sweet dreams, bunnies.